Nancy's Little One

A Lesbian Mommy Domme trains her baby girl in the MDLG kink

by Tina Moore

Table of Content

Chapter 1

Loren was not like most girls her age. At 25, she had no interest in getting married and starting a family. Loren didn't care about where her friends went on holidays, and she certainly didn't care about what was going on in the world around her. She was content living her predictable life while feeling so dangerously lonely it made her heart hurt. Loren worked as a real-estate agent and spent her week showing wealthy couples around luxury mansions she knew she would never want as her own. With the marble baths and indoor swimming pools, gardens greener than one in central park and more tech than she truly knew what to do with, these mansions were divine but soulless. They reminded her of herself. She had been working for the company for five years, and within those five years, she had learned one thing. Rich people liked expensive price tags. If a mansion was selling for 15 million, she would bump the price to 20, if a property was selling for 35, she bumped it to 40. Due to her excellent selling style, she had made a powerful reputation in the real-estate game, winning countless awards and enjoying the high commission. However, her success, she suspected, had nothing to do with her sales pitch. Her clients didn't need convincing to buy the mansions. The decision on the property was already made, that was not what they desired. It was her. With a girlish vulnerability yet eyes that screamed use me, there had not been too many clients which she had not fucked. It wasn't that she was a slut. It was that she couldn't feel the world. She used these clients as much as they used her. The game both were trying to win, the prize, power. She wasn't even straight, but that didn't matter to her. Sex was sex. She would let a husband fuck her arse from behind while he choked her as she was cuddled and lovingly teased by a wife. An exciting mix of hate fucking and motherly love was the closest thing to what she truly desired, and although it never lasted more than a night, it was all she had.

As she showed a new client to the open air cinema, she felt a hand gently stroke on the small of her back.

"And from here you will be able to see the ocean," Loren explained as the hand reached under her skirt. Loren spread her thighs slightly to encourage the groping hand of the rich women. The woman moved in front of Loren. Her eyes sparkled with desire, but Loren's were dead. The older woman didn't seem to care as she began to stroke Loren's warm pussy through her satin panties.

"It's unusual for me only to show a property to one party. Will your husband be joining us?" Loren asked the woman 15 years her senior.

"Not unless you want him to," the woman replied, moving

Loren's panties to the side and sliding a finger into her aching wet cunt. Loren moaned and buckled over, holding the taller woman's shoulder for support.

"There, there little one, come over here," the woman said as she felt for the chair behind her and sat down. She pulled Loren on of her lap, making the younger woman straddle her womanly thighs as she was fucked. Enjoying the breathless moans of the compliant girl, the woman leaned back and took in her beauty.

"You're going to be a good girl for me. You'll enjoy the commission you receive from my husband buying this house," she said as she pumped her fingers inside Loren harder, rubbing her thumb over her clit and making her rock her hips and grind down on the woman's hand.

"That's it," the woman coaxed as Loren leaned forward and wrapped her arms around the woman's neck. Loren closed her eyes and gasped as she came, cum dripping down her thighs and over the woman's hand.

"My my you are a dirty little girl," the woman said as she slowly took her fingers from Loren's juicy pussy and began to undo her blouse.

"Do you know what dirty little girls need?" She asked Loren who was enjoying the sight of this woman's breasts too much to bother replying. Slap. The woman hit Loren's face with a force that sent her head falling back. The older woman had held

Loren in place with her other arm as she slapped her, clearly aware of her strength.

"I'm waiting for a reply sweet pea," the woman said as she unclipped her black lace bra.

"Um, no, I don't know what dirty little girls like me need," Loren said, playing the woman's game.

"They need a Mommy," the woman replied, grabbing the back of Loren's hair and drawing her mouth to her nipple. Loren could feel the sun burning through the back of her light pink blouse. It was her favorite one. Something about this blouse drove women wild. She had worn it on purpose.

"Do you want me to be your Mommy baby girl?" The older woman said in a friendly voice, Loren had not heard from her before. Loren didn't know what she should say. She was happy her mouth of full of this woman's nipple because it meant she didn't have to respond. She just nodded her head and continued to nurse.

"Yes, good girl. I knew you needed me," the older woman said as she gently rocked her, stroking her hair while Loren closed her eyes and suckled. She hadn't even realized she'd fallen asleep until she woke up. She was not outside anymore, and the woman was gone. She recognized the room, though. It was one of the rooms in the mansion. Loren looked down and saw her clothes were still on, but her heels had been taken off. Beside her on the nightstand was a glass of water and a note. It read, 'Thank you for showing me the property. I'll be in touch'. *Doubt it,* Loren thought. *Now I have to explain why I was so long with one client. Usually, this shit happens the first night they move in.* Loren was happy she had not scheduled any other appointments for the day. She checked her phone and saw that it was 4:30 in the afternoon. She'd hit traffic getting back to the office, and it would take her an extra half an hour to get home.

Chapter 2

It was a week after she had shown that woman the property she woke up suddenly as her phone rang. Loren looked at the name on the phone and rolled her eyes as she answered.

"What the hell did you do?" Came a screaming woman down the phone. Loren's eyes popped open from the sleep she just ripped out of and looked at the clock. *5:30 in the morning, this bitch is going to ring me at 5:30 in the morning?* Loren thought as she played dumb.

"What are you talking about?" She replied, trying to wake up.

"I'm talking about the fact that you, I can't even believe this!" Loren's boss exclaimed.

"That I what Jen!?" Loren shouted back down the phone angry her boss wasn't getting to the point.

"That you closed the deal 15 mill over the asking price!" Jen stated happily.

15 mill over the asking price. She wasn't lying; I'll enjoy this commission very much, Loren thought to herself.

"Yo, you still there or have you died of shock?" Jen asked.

"Yeah, I'm here. Holy shit. Fuck yes. You better give me that pay rise now, lady!" Loren said, laughing.

"How much money do you need, you just landed the biggest fish we have ever caught. You'll be looking for your department soon!" Jen replied.

"I'll talk to you about the details later. I'm going back to sleep, and I'm not coming in today," Loren stated before she hung up the phone quickly as to not hear Jen's rebuttal.

Loren lay in bed. She thought about the woman. She couldn't even remember her name. *Suzan, Sharon, Sandra? Who the fuck cares, I just got paid*, Loren thought as she rolled over and took out her notebook and pen.

Ever changing nature and forced normalization silences scream in the throes of torturing stillness. To look upon a dancer so graced and elegant as she moves on broken legs yet only to her ears, the sound of crushing bone can be heard. How wonderful a sight she must be with her form and expression, oh but the unwavering admiration that is laid around her neck only serves as her collar and leash. The pulling from another, she moves into the positions they desire and kept there with a promise of...love. It's beautiful they say as they watched her fit into their boxes, pushing her shattered limbs into the shapes of their cages.

She read over her work and smiled a sad smile. That woman had been the closest thing to kindness Loren had felt in a long time, and she couldn't even remember her name. Deciding to go to the gym, she got up and walked over to her cupboard. Looking through her clothes, she remembered the first time she had bought a designer shirt. Five years on and designer clothes weren't exciting anymore. She found a pair of navy track pants and a white crop top. She laced up her newest pair of runners and put her hair up in a messy ponytail. She looked at herself in the mirror. She ran her fingers over her abs and tweaked her hair so that it fell more to the left side. She liked that her tits were small enough only to need a sports crop; at a B-cup she didn't have to worry about much bounce. She walked out of her room, grabbed her gym bag, and walked down the steps of her home and on the street.

The street always made her heart happy. The smell of hot dogs and the flurry of birds as they fought over a piece of scrap a child would undoubtedly be throwing. The trees which dotted the sidewalks littered the ground. Mostly she liked how invisible she could become. No one knew she was there, and no one would notice if she were gone. It was a comforting thought.

When Loren got to the gym, it was unusually quiet.

"Slow morning Rach?" Loren asked the girl who checked in everyone.

"Yeah, I don't know what's going on. You're looking ripped!" Rach replied, taking in Loren's body. Loren looked down; she knew she looked good.

"Thanks," she said, laughing as she walked into the changing room. There was no-one else in the changing room as Loren put her bag in her locker and stretched on the bench. Her toned legs extending elegantly and her arms reaching over to hold her toes made her feel flexible even though she wasn't.

"I thought I might find you here," said a voice behind her. Loren quickly turned her head to see that the woman from the mansion, the one who had given her a noteworthy commission was standing in work out gear behind her.

"Mo — um, Hi," Loren said more excitedly than she would have liked. The woman smiled and stroked Loren's cheek, making her blush.

"Sweet girl, you can call me mommy if you like," she replied, making Loren blush harder. Loren looked around anxiously; hoping no-one could hear the other woman. She didn't know what to say, so she just looked down and toyed with her shoelaces.

"My husband would like to meet you. He is very grateful you found such a wonderful home for us," the older woman stated. *I don't want to meet him. I don't care how fucking happy he is. I want you*, Loren thought to herself.

"I can't, I'm busy," she said when she finally spoke. The older woman sat down next to her and pulled her into her arms lovingly.

"Not right now silly, tonight," she said as she kissed Loren's forehead. 'This is too much. I'm done', Loren told herself as she pushed the other woman away.

"I said I'm not interested in your fucking husband," Loren

half shouted as she walked to the door and out into the weight room.

Chapter 3

"Rich people are the worst. They are all fake, and none of them even care about you. It's like you're just a thing for them to use and throw away," Loren said to Nancy who was wondering how many more times Loren, and she would have this conversation. Nancy owned the trendy café across the street from Loren's apartment, and ever since that first day she moved into the neighborhood she had come to Nancy's. The pie was all she was after on those bad days. Nancy would always find a way to break through Loren's cold, distant eyes and soothe the little pieces of a broken heart that Loren tried so hard to hide. Nancy was born to Latina parents who gave her the whitest name they could think of before adopting her out, or so said Nancy. But her name suited her. She had the whole motherly thing down, and her cuddly body with wide hips and full heavy breasts often made Loren wet just sitting in her spot at the counter sharing her problems. But it wasn't just Loren who got excited by Nancy. The way she wore her long thick wavy hair made most people who came into her diner stay longer than they needed too. Taking in her full lips and eyes that could melt a cold heart in moments, Loren looked at Nancy for a reply.

"Well yeah, you've been saying that for years," Nancy said

as she poured Loren another coffee and wiped her hands on the apron, she had tied to her waist over her ripped jeans. Despite her 45 years of age, Nancy looked no older than 30. Her fashion sense of urban cool and timeless class often made Loren wonder just how successful she indeed was. From the stories Nancy had told Loren, Loren wondered why she would still be working five days a week.

"Why do you even mess with them? What are you looking for?" Nancy added. Loren wished she could tell her what she was looking for.

"I don't know Nancy, nothing I guess," Loren lied. Nancy suspected as much, but she ignored Loren's attempt to mask a blindingly obvious truth and tried to turn the conversation homebound.

"I'll leave in about an hour. If you want, we could hang out at mine. I've got movies and popcorn?" Nancy said as she smiled kindly at Loren. *Fuck it,* Loren thought to herself.

"Alright," she said as she took out her phone and waited for Nancy to finish work. Inside Nancy's living room Loren sat nervously.

"Your home is charming," Loren stated, looking around. With white wooden floorboards and white walls, the house looked light and airy. Nancy had a wall length wooden bench on one wall and a thick black fake fur rug covering the better part of the living room floor. Colorful artworks hung from the walls, and her TV was mounted to a wall. Loren was sitting on a dark green suede couch and thought the color combination of match black armchairs on either side where cool. *Coming here was a mistake, fuck, where am I going to get pie now?* She thought as Nancy came back with the popcorn and handed a bowl to Loren, noting the fear in her sweet eyes, Nancy sat away from her.

"Don't worry, I'm not going to get too close to you," she said reassuringly as if reading Loren's mind. Loren just smiled and looked down, embarrassed that after four years of talking to Nancy, she had her figured out. The movie started, and Loren was hooked. She loved that film did that to her. She got completely drawn in and felt as though she was experiencing what the characters on the screen where.

"Um, where's your bathroom, Nancy?" Loren said, breaking the silence between them.

"Oh, it's just down the hall, to the right," Nancy replied, giving hand directions. Loren smiled and got up and followed the instructions. As she was coming back to the living room, she noticed something that caught her eye, a fluffy pink rug. Loren walked into the room carefully, not to make the door creak and was overwhelmed. It was a nursery and not a nursery you'd find at a baby shower. There was an adult sized cot, a rocking chair that looked custom-made for two adults and a bookcase filled with the kind of books Loren never let herself read. Toys in a toy box in the corner of the room and handcuffs bolted into the wall.

She was so overcome with what she saw Loren didn't hear Nancy come up behind her.

"This isn't why I invited you around Loren. Let me shut the door," Nancy warmly said as she took Loren's hand and gently led her out of the room, shutting the door behind her. Loren didn't know where to look she certainly didn't want to look at Nancy.

"Are you alright?" Nancy asked tenderly, still holding Loren's hand. Loren just nodded her head and walked back to the living room and sat on the sofa. Nancy sat in the same chair she had previously been sitting in and turned the movie back on. Loren wasn't interested in the film anymore. Her breathing was shallow, and she was almost in tears. It was too much to know that Nancy was some sort of caregiver. It was too much to know that Nancy knew Loren wanted it. It was all just too much. The kindness Loren had been looking for had been in front of her the whole time, and she never knew. Nancy never tried anything, and god knows the times Loren had turned up drunk at the café Nancy could have had full access. But she never did, she would always just give Loren something to eat and walk her home, tucking her in and stroking her forehead as she fell asleep.
Loren looked at Nancy, who was already looking at her.

"So, what's that about?" Loren asked nervously.

"I'm into kink. I identify as a Mommy Domme. I like to have a submissive who I can take care of," Nancy said in an almost clinical way as she tried not to scare Loren off. Nancy was already surprised at how long Loren had stayed after seeing the nursery. She knew Loren was a runner. From the stories Loren had shared with her over the years, Nancy was sure she would have been out the door by now.

"Oh. That's cool," Loren said nodding as she spoke trying to be at ease.

"Loren. You don't need to feel uncomfortable; it's not meant for you. You should know by now you can trust me. As if I'd do anything to you," Nancy said as she stood up and paused the movie. She came over and sat next to Loren, happy she didn't flinch at the closeness but very aware she was forcing herself not to.

"Am I not what you like? I get it, like, not many people want me like long-term," Loren asked, looking down, wanting more than anything for Nancy not to say it was because Loren was unappealing. Nancy took Loren's hands in hers and kissed them, meeting her surprised eyes and holding contact.

"You are stunning, but I'm not a monster sweet girl. I can see you're hurting and I wouldn't get off on using your pain just to get what I want," Nancy said as she stroked Loren's hands with her thumbs.

"I wish you would," Loren said quietly as a tear rolled down her cheek looking away ashamed. She looked up at Nancy with her aqua green eyes filled with tears.

"I wish you were a monster like everyone else and I wish you would just take me how you wanted to," Loren repeated as she broke away from Nancy and walked out the door.

Chapter 4

Loren stayed away from the diner for months. She would see Nancy as she crossed the street to walk to work or when she came home, but she didn't go into the diner. She had lost a bit of weight since she stopped eating pie and decided that it was for the best. Nancy had seen her too. Out the back of the diner where she would occasionally have a cigarette, Nancy could watch Loren work out in the park. Her healthy, slender body dripping in sweat glistening in the midday sun made Nancy wet thinking of what she would do with her.

On a cold winter's afternoon, Loren had left work early to come home. She was frustrated with how the clients treated her and decided to go for a run to blow off some steam. Turning the corner towards home, she noticed a large group of men walking towards her. As she was about to pass the diner, she put her head down and hoped they wouldn't say anything to her.

"Oh hello beautiful," one man jeered, grabbing his dick and biting his bottom lip.

"Give us a smile," another one said as he blocked Loren's path, refusing to let her pass. They began to circle her, and as she frantically looked for an escape, she locked eyes with Nancy.

Nancy saw Loren's scared eyes through the frosted window, and it made her blood boil. She came storming out in the middle of winter in just her gray woolen dress, her 6'4" height taking the men by surprise. She grabbed the closest one she could find and pulled him back, making him fall onto the cold hard ground.

"Get the fuck away from her," she yelled as she reached in and grabbed Loren's hand, pulling her into a warm embrace before turning her around and pushing her into the diner. Nancy didn't say a word but led Loren to the back room and wrapped her large jacket around Loren's shivering body.

"Thanks, it's OK, I'll go," Loren said as she stood to leave.

"Sit," Nancy commanded in a voice Loren had never heard before. Wide-eyed Loren involuntarily sat.

"You aren't going anywhere you hear me. We have played this game long enough. You said you wanted me. Well, you've got me, which means you're going to do exactly as I say, understood?" Nancy said sternly as she handed Loren a cup of warm cocoa.

"OK Nancy," Loren said softly, looking into the cup at the small pink marshmallows bobbing in the warm liquid. Nancy smiled in satisfaction and came to sit beside Loren. She wrapped her arm around the smaller girl, and Loren sighed and gave in, resting her head on Nancy's full breast.

"I've missed you," Loren said quietly, surrender in the voice, melting Nancy's heart.

"I have never…it's only ever been bad… I don't know what I'm supposed to do. I don't want to make you mad," Loren nervously stammered.

"I know you've been a big girl for so long, but Mommy's here now, and I'm going to take care of you," Nancy reassured Loren as she stroked her cheek with her other hand.

"I've read about contracts and stuff," Loren tried to say as Nancy gently placed her thumb in Loren's mouth to silence her.

"Didn't I just say to let Mommy take care of it? We are sitting in a broom cupboard baby, this is not the time to be writing contracts," Nancy replied, getting wetter than she had been in months.

"Sorry, Mommy," Loren softly replied as she continued sucking Nancy's thumb. Nancy smiled with satisfaction; it hadn't taken Loren any time at all to start calling her Mommy instead of Nancy. *She just needs love; she's perfectly trainable*, Nancy thought to herself.

"Drink that, and I'll take you home. I've finished for the day," Nancy said, taking her thumb out of Loren's mouth so that she could drink the last of her cocoa.

Nancy loved that Loren reached for her hand as they made their way to Loren's apartment. She let Loren open the door and followed Loren inside. She had been inside Loren's apartment multiple times before, but never like this. Seeing that Loren didn't know what to do or what headspace to be in, Nancy called her over. She patted the spot on the couch next to her and tilted her head, telling Loren all she needed to know as she quickly walked over and sat down.

"So here it is sweetheart. I know you have your big fancy job. I respect that. Hell, I'm glad you've been able to support yourself for so long and so well. I'm not going to uproot your whole life, just yet. When do you think you could stay at my house? I want to start with making sure we want the same basics," Nancy said while holding a shivering Loren. The house was warm, but Loren was nervous.

"I finish work at 6. I don't do anything after that. Sometimes there's a gala or something, but I've gotten out of going before. I can stay tonight, what basics?" Loren said cautiously.

"You don't have to get out of those events unless you want to. Work is work, sweetheart; everyone's got to eat. OK good, we can see how tonight goes and take it from there. Basics like, make sure we want the same things dynamically, sexually, and emotionally. It's just like a trail to see if we mesh," Nancy explained.

"OK, Mommy," she said as she melted into Nancy's big loving arms. Before jumping up suddenly as she had a thought.

"So, sex?" Loren asked.

"What about it?" Nancy laughed.

"Well, do I still get it?" Loren questioned.

"I'll fuck you when I want you. If you're lucky and you do what I ask, when and how I want something done baby girl I might even use it as a reward. Your pussy is mine now, and if I'm not happy with you, you can stay in chastity all month-long for all I care," Nancy answered, rubbing Loren's pussy through her workout tights. Loren made soft, breathless sounds as she closed her eyes and let Nancy continued to rub her, feeling her caress get firmer and a finger poke her pussy through her tights made Loren flinch backward.

"Don't run from me baby," Nancy said lovingly but with a clear warning. Loren held her breath and slowly moved back to where Nancy's hand was, letting her touch what she wanted to touch. Before long Loren was breathing shallow and fast. Just as she was about to cum, Nancy stopped, and Loren opened her eyes, compliant written in her eyes. Loren had already learned it was better to stay quiet than to complain to Nancy.

"You aren't allowed to cum just yet princess," Nancy said as she got up and pulled Loren up with her. They went into Loren's bedroom and packed the clothes she would need for the night and next morning. Nancy opened Loren's pantry and looked at the sugary foods she had stockpiled.

"How you keep that little body of yours while pumping it with this shit I will never know. You're going to be very moody as I wean you off this crap," Nancy said, looking at Loren and reaching out to feel her little waist.

"Well, yeah. I don't know. I eat what tastes good," Loren said. Nancy looked at her and smiled wickedly.

"No, you haven't, but you're about to," Nancy said as she leaned against Loren's kitchen table and slowly spread her legs.

"Here, now," Nancy commanded as she clicked her fingers to the floor where she wanted Loren. Obediently Loren knelt before Nancy and ran her hands under Nancy's dress.

"Make Mommy happy baby girl," Nancy said as Loren pulled down her panties and saw Nancy's perfect pussy for the first time. Her lips were full and puffy, with a thick strip of black hair that stopped just before her clit which pushed out eagerly. Nancy watched as Loren took it all in and smiled with satisfaction and desire.

"Kiss me there, baby," Nancy directed, mesmerizing Loren. She quickly dived on Nancy's pussy and kissed her lips, parting them with her tongue as she breathed through her mouth. She sucked on her clit and felt Nancy's hand come under her dress and hold Loren's head there. Moaning and gently fucking Loren's face. Loren flicked her tongue over Nancy's flick and then sucked it hard, enjoying the feeling of Nancy becoming wetter as juices pressed against her mouth. Nancy was right; she did taste sweet.

"Yes, good girl," Nancy moaned as she came loudly, shaking as she squirted into Loren's mouth, making her choke at the unexpected liquid flowing down her throat.

"I'm sorry little girl," Nancy said as she heard Loren coughing.

"Did Mommy cum down that pretty little throat of yours?" Nancy asked as she picked Loren up and made her straddle one of her thighs. She rubbed Loren's back and patted her firmly, and Loren snuggled into Nancy's breasts and sucked her thumb.

"Yes, Mommy," Loren said, trying not to cough.

"I liked it though Mommy," quickly followed as Loren became nervous she would upset Nancy by coughing.

"Good sweetheart, Mommy liked it too," Nancy said, picking Loren up like the baby she was and carried her to the couch. She sat down and placed Loren on her lap.

"I hope you've got a hungry tummy baby girl," Nancy said as she took off her dress revealing two massive breasts. Loren's eyes grew wide as she saw Nancy's breasts overflow out of her bra and was even happier when Nancy took her off. Her nipples were hard and thick, perfect for sucking. Loren nodded and smiled as Nancy took her thumb out of her mouth and replaced it with her nipple, pushing into Loren's mouth by the weight of her heavy breast.

"Suck little one, let's fill that little tummy of yours," Nancy said as warm milk flowed into Loren's mouth much to her surprise. She tried to pull away surprised that Nancy's breasts were full of milk, but Nancy held her breast firmly to Loren's lips, keeping her head in place with her other hand.

"Don't get fussy now baby girl. Mommy doesn't want to have to spank you," Nancy said warningly. Loren stopped squirming and opened her mouth wide as Nancy squirted milk into her pretty mouth. After a while, Loren held Nancy's breast in her hands, and Nancy stroked her tummy, enjoy seeing the slight swelling of it being filled. The night was setting in, and Nancy knew she wanted Loren in the nursery before she got too sleepy. She could see Loren's eyes fluttering shut as she looked up at Nancy who was aware there was still the matter of bathing and diapering Loren before she could let her fall asleep.

"That's enough, sweetheart," Nancy said warmly as she took Loren's hands off her and put her dress back on. Loren frowned slightly, her lips forming a cute pout. Not the bratty kind Nancy hated but the sweet, sleepy kind. She picked up Loren's bags and led her out the door.

Chapter 5

"Go to the bathroom baby, Mommy will run a bath for you in a minute," Nancy said as they entered her home. Loren nodded sleepily and headed to the bathroom. After Nancy put her bags in her room, she walked down the hallway and saw Loren was standing in the middle of the room, sucking her thumb and clutching her bunny by the ear.

"Come here, baby," Nancy said as she opened her arms to Loren who practically fell into them. Nancy held Loren up as she undressed her and ran her a bath. Nancy liked that Loren became doe-eyed and non-verbal when she was sleepy rather than the bratty hyperactive girls she had in the past. She washed Loren's small, thin body and made her giggle when she rubbed her between her legs. Helping Loren out of the bath she dried her. Nancy led her to the nursery and felt her hand being pulled back as Loren stopped promptly.

"What is it little one?" Nancy asked, slightly concerned. Loren looked as afraid as she had the first time she had seen it. It had not been six hours since Nancy had claimed Loren as her own and the thought that maybe she was rushing Loren only crossed her mind now.

"I don't think I like this. I don't want to dress in lame baby clothes. I'm too cool for those; it's not my style," Loren whispered into Nancy's ear.

"No? What is your style then baby because you haven't even seen what I have for you," Nancy asked as she sat down on the floor and pulled Loren down to sit in her lap.

"Wait, what, you've got me things? You've planned this?" Loren asked as she stopped playing with Nancy's hair.

"Ever since you walked out on me little one, did you think Mommy was going to give you up that easily?" Nancy asked, holding Loren's hand firmly in place, making Loren's stomach tighten. Loren thought back to that day and remembered how Nancy said the nursery wasn't for her.

"But you said it wasn't for me," she stated, looking at Nancy for an explanation.

"It wasn't, but it is now," Nancy replied, rubbing over the front of Loren's sports tights.

"Please, can I just have a t-shirt and panties?" Loren asked, her eyes begging.

Please Mommy," Nancy corrected patting Loren's pussy firmly making her jump.

"Please, Mommy, just a t-shirt and panties," Loren begged.

"I'll compromise on a t-shirt, but you'll wear a diaper pretty baby, you don't wear big girl panties when you are not at work," Nancy said as she stood up and lifted Loren on the changing table. Loren looked around trying to focus on something, on anything. She wanted this, badly. But how could she give in to it? It was like Nancy knew what she was thinking about as she soothed Loren's worried mind.

"You will love this little one. I know you will. You'll be Mommy's cute little girl, don't you want that?" Nancy asked stroking Loren's forehead until she stopped frowning.

"Yes, Mommy, but what if I feel silly," Loren asked honestly.

"No one is going to see you, baby, no one is going to think you look silly, I certainly don't think you look silly. You don't like to be picked on, do you, sweetie?" Nancy asked, noting that humiliating Loren was off the table. Over the years, she had learned a lot about the type of things Loren liked; the concept of humiliation never came up.

"OK, Mommy," Loren replied nervously as she scrunched up her toes. Nancy gave her a fluffy pink blanket to snuggle into and pushed a white pacifier into her mouth and kissed her cheeks before she powered Loren for the first time. Tightening the diaper around her small waist, Nancy felt proud to have a baby girl as adorable as Loren. 'Mine at last,' Nancy thought, remembering who she had watched Loren over the years and pictured her just like this, lying there finally dependent on her. Sitting Loren up, she looked down to touch the diaper, running her hands over the crinkly plastic material. Nancy smiled as she walked to the cupboard and let Loren choose out of two t-shirts, something she would never have allowed another baby do. But she figured if allowing Loren have half a say in what she wore was going to keep her happy and Nancy's baby, it was worth the compromise. Loren smiled and pointed to a dark maroon shirt, and Nancy took out a plain white cotton diaper cover and black knee-high socks. She liked how tight the diaper cover was and rubbed Loren's pussy through the padding admiring how sweet she looked as she squirmed with the new sensation.

"Give me your little feet. I don't want you to get cold leggys baby," Nancy said as she rolled up the socks.

"There, come here, princess," Nancy said as she opened her arms and lifted Loren on the changing table. At 5'6" and only 60kg, Loren was easy for Nancy to carry. Nancy patted Loren's padded bottom as she took her to the living room floor. She placed Loren gently down, passed her her blankie and bunny and turned on a movie she knew Loren would love before going to have a shower. When Nancy came out of the shower, Loren was wrapped up in her blankie and fast asleep, her paci lying next to her. Nancy smiled and went to the fridge to make something for dinner. As she cooked, she looked over at her sweet girl stirring in her sleep. *Probably getting used to the new noises and the smell of a real meal*, Nancy thought to herself. She brought her dinner over to the sofa and picked Loren up and placed her on the couch. Nancy turned on the TV and rubbed Loren's back while she ate. Just before Nancy finished her meal,

Loren sleepily stirred and woke herself up with a fright.

"It's OK baby girl, you're safe, you're at my house," Nancy said lovingly as Loren looked around the room almost teary eyed. She turned her head until she found Nancy and crawled to her.

"You want to cuddle with Mommy?" Nancy said she put Loren's pacifier back into her mouth. As Loren nodded yes, Nancy moved her plate out the way and wrapped Loren in her arms as Loren's tummy grumbled.

"I'm hungry, Mommy," Loren quietly stated.

"What are you eating? Can I please have some Mommy?" She asked sweetly.

"It's only spaghetti baby. Do you want me to make you something else?" Nancy asked.

"Nope, I like sketti Mommy," Loren replied as her tummy grumbled again.

"You'd probably like anything right now," Nancy said as she got up and served Loren a bowl of pasta.

"Thank you, Mommy," Loren said as she reached for the bowl. Nancy had every intention of feeding her, but Loren had instinctively thought she would feed herself. *In time*, Nancy said realizing Loren had not done it on purpose, only out of habit.

"Yes, baby girl," Nancy answered, turning the TV off.

"It's about work. You know what I've done with clients. What happens if someone tried something?" Loren asked as worry spread across her face.

"Princess, when have you ever wanted to be with any of them?" Nancy asked in return, already knowing the answer.

"Never," Loren said, looking down at her bowl.

"Well, then. Don't let them," Nancy replied.

"I don't know how to do that, Mommy," Loren replied helplessly. Nancy thought, *that is true. I don't know how many times I've wiped her tears away after she let someone fuck her.*

"OK, tell you what. If someone tries something, ring me, straight away. Do you even need that job? Maybe you should find one a little less, tactile?" Nancy said.

"No I don't need the job, I have enough savings to not work for years. I don't think I even like the job, I just do it because, well, it's something to do," Loren replied honestly.

"Yeah I know baby girl, come here," Nancy said as she took Loren's bowl and opened her arms finding Loren in them within seconds.

"Can we just try it and see what happens? Maybe because I have you now it'll be different," Loren stated.

"It better be. I'm not sharing you with anyone. That's a big rule for me, Loren. You're my good girl, no one else's," Nancy said, making Loren's tummy churn. After an afternoon and evening being called her baby girl, hearing Nancy call her by her first name sounded awful.

"I don't want to be anyone else's, Mommy," Loren said as

she fell asleep again in Nancy's safe, loving arms.

Chapter 6

The next morning Loren woke before Nancy and got dressed in her work clothes. She looked in the mirror and felt her headspace shift into the mindset of an independent woman. Walking out into the living room and around to the kitchen, she made herself a cup of coffee and walked out to the veranda. Below the world looked like it did every other morning, but for Loren, it couldn't have felt different. She felt different. Nancy was different. Hearing footsteps behind her, she turned around to see Nancy walking over to her. Her black satin pajamas shining as the light touched them.

"Good morning," Nancy whispered into Loren's ear as she kissed her cheek. Nancy took the time to look Loren up and down, noting that she was far from the sweet baby girl who fell asleep in her arms last night. Loren's tight egg-shell blue dress and her cream pump heels complemented her light skin and white blonde hair. Her baby blue eyes sparkled in the morning sun, and the wind made the stray hairs in her ponytail fly.

"Hi," Loren replied, unsure of what to do or say next. Turning to face away from Nancy Loren sipped her coffee and walked back inside. Nancy followed her, wondering if she had pushed Loren too far the previous night.

"Hey," Nancy affectionately said as she grabbed Loren's arm. Loren looked at her blankly before pulling away and looking out the window.

"I hope you don't mind that I got dressed and stuff. I just wasn't sure if you were working today or like, what your plans were and I didn't want to wake you if you weren't working cause like, it's your sleep in but I have to be at work in like 35 minutes, so I just thought I'd go. And am I allowed just to go. I don't know what I'm doing Mommy. Nancy? What do I call you during the day? Is it OK if I call you Mommy during the day?" Loren tumbled her words out in one highly stressed breathe, and Nancy leaned against the kitchen counter and folded her arms across her chest, getting comfortable while she listened to Loren's long rambling. As Loren noticed Nancy's amused look on her face, she stopped and bashfully looked at Nancy wanting all her questions answered.

"Are you sure that's everything?" Nancy laughed leaning forward to take Loren's hand and pull her into a loving embrace.

"Yeah, for now at least," Loren giggled as she kissed Nancy's lips.

"You can call me Mommy or Nancy during the day sweetheart. If I call you and you are with a client or colleagues, I don't expect you to call me Mommy. But the minute you walk into that door regardless of what you are wearing, you'd want to be calling me Mommy. In the mornings, of course, get yourself dressed, get whatever you want to eat for breakfast and do whatever you need to do to get into the headspace for work. I think it is important for you to keep some of those things to do for yourself, if you feel like you want me to do them for you, let me know. But for now, you've been taking care of yourself for so long; it would be way too much if I took over everything," Nancy replied while stroking Loren's freshly straightened hair.

"OK, Mommy," Loren said, taking a moment to take it all in. As her phone alarm began to ring, signaling she needed to leave for work, Loren looked at Nancy, aware she was not meant to pull away from her.

"Go, sweetheart, don't be upset if I don't message you during the day, I'm going to the spa today and then having a friend over for coffee. I'll see you sometime before 7?" Nancy asked gently squeezing Loren before letting her go, following her into her bedroom as she collected her bag.

"Oh, have a fun time! It sounds like you've got a great day planned Mommy!" Loren exclaimed as she headed to the door.

"I liked kissing you, Mommy," Loren whispered as she opened the door to leave, looking back at Nancy expectantly.

"Are you trying to get me to kiss you now, baby? I wouldn't recommend you try to tell me what to do young lady; it won't serve you well," Nancy corrected making Loren blush and her stomach churn.

"Please Mommy, can I kiss you goodbye?" Loren said,

begging this time instead of trying to manipulate.

"Better. That'll be something we work on," Nancy said as she patted the side of Loren's face, slightly frustrated she couldn't punish her that very moment. Holding Loren close, Nancy kissed her full on the lips. Impressed with herself when she felt Loren's legs buckle underneath her, Nancy quickly wrapped an arm around Loren's waist to hold her up. Nancy ran her fingers through the smaller woman's hair, causing Loren to moan and push herself harder into Nancy's enveloping body.

"Go to work baby girl. Mommy will see you later," Nancy said, breaking the kiss and watching her princess walk away. Closing the door behind her, Nancy sighed. She had not had a full-time baby in years and had forgotten how challenging developing a routine and dynamic could be. It was different when a girl had come over to be babied for the evening. That was all the same excitement level. This type of domination was different. It was highs and lows, exciting and boring. Nancy looked to where Loren had left her coffee cup and frowned. *The dishwasher was only 3" away Loren*; Nancy thought to herself as she took out a pen and paper and began writing a list of things she needed to teach Loren. It was hardly Loren's fault, and Nancy knew she wouldn't punish Loren for things she had not even informed her.

Focus, Loren said to herself as she walked a new set of clients around the indoor pool area of her biggest deal of the week. The couple, somewhere in their 30s, had told Loren they had picked her as their contact after being recommended by a couple she closed a deal with last year. She had tried to smile at their comment, knowing that this would probably not end well.

"Show us the bedroom again Loren," the stern-voiced man commanded. Knowingly, Loren led them to the master bedroom, which overlooked the city. She opened the door to them but stayed in the corridor. Watching as the man and his new bride walked circles in the room, pretending to look at its features.

"Won't you join us? I have a question about the ceiling," the man said, his hands shifting to the pockets of his tailored trousers. Loren slowly walked into the room, and the woman circled behind her. The man stood firm in his place, next to the bed and looking up at the high ceiling.

"What would you like to know about it?" Loren said, trying to sound professional and not afraid.

"I want to know if you like the look of it," the man said as he grabbed Loren's wrist and pushed her onto the bed. Jumping on top of her quickly and pinning her hips down with his, pushing his hard cock onto her silk panties as he pulled up her matching colored dress.

"Get the fuck off me," Loren yelled as his bride came over to the bed and began caressing Loren's breasts.

"We were told you like it. That you're the filthy little slut who puts out to make the deal," the man said as he wrapped a hand around Loren's neck and squeezed.

"Stay nice and quiet for me, bitch. Or I'll fuck that pretty mouth of yours until your jaw hurts," he added unzipping his pants. Pulling out his hard cock, Loren could see the pre-cum dripping onto her panties. As he forced her legs apart, his wife began to kiss Loren, biting her lip and making her pull away in pain. The man ran his wet cock up and down Loren's panty clad pussy, pushing it into her pussy and arse.

"Mm, which one first," he mocked as he rubbed her mound firmly. Loren stopped fighting and became still. She closed her eyes and thought of Nancy as tears rolled down onto her cheeks.

"Open that whore mouth of yours bitch, I'm going pump you full of cock, and you're going to be my cum slut," he said taking his hand and forcing Loren's mouth open.

"Um, they never said anything about her crying," the wife said to her husband as she stopped kissing Loren's neck and looked at her face.

"I don't want this," Loren whispered, her eyes still shut and tears again rolling down her face.

"Oh, fuck. I'm so sorry; they just said you liked to be taken like this. Fuck, sorry," the man said as he put his dick back into his pants. The woman grabbed his hand and led him quickly out of the room.

"We'll buy the house, don't worry. You don't need to go to the police or anything," he said as they left the room. Loren waited until she heard the front doors slam and their car drive away and slowly opened her eyes. She took her panties off and pulled her dress down, not wanting to have any trace of that man on her. She went to the bathroom and looked at herself in the mirror. Her makeup was smudged beyond repair. Her hair was in disarray, and she had dark red markings around her throat. Her lips where she had been bitten were also red and swollen, and she only had one thing on her mind, Mommy.

As Loren strolled towards Nancy's house, she thought of the one rule Nancy had made crystal clear, she was not to be shared. Did this count? It's not like Loren had encouraged it. *What am I supposed to say to her? Did I fuck up the on the first day? Was it even my fault?* Loren asked as she disappeared into the crowd of people exiting the subway. As she approached Nancy's building, she took her panties out of her bag and threw them into the trash and headed inside. The foyer was quiet, and for the first time, Loren felt a warm feeling about going somewhere, which felt like home. *For how long?* Loren thought as she climbed the two flights of stairs and rummaged through her bag to find the keys. Opening the door and walking inside, Loren knew Nancy wasn't home. She put her bag neatly in the corner of Nancy's room and took off her dress, making a mental note to burn it.

Walking through the house naked, she found her phone and called Jen.

"Hi, it's me," Loren said plainly.

"I quit," she added quickly.

"What?" Jen half shouted down the phone.

"I quit. Pay me what I'm owed, I can't do this anymore," Loren said as she hung up the phone and deleted Jen's number. Throwing her phone on the couch, Loren walked into the bathroom and turned on the shower. Letting the hot water burn her skin, she thought about how she was going to tell Nancy what had happened today. Loren sat on the couch for the rest of the day and watched as the hours ticked by, hoping that Nancy would come home early. To her surprise at 4:15, she heard the key in the lock open, and Nancy walked in, surprised to see Loren as another woman followed her inside. Luckily for Loren, she had decided to put clothes back on an hour earlier. Her white short shorts and orange singlet caught Nancy off guard as Loren's nipples were visible through the thin material.

"Oh I'm sorry, I didn't know you were having guests, um," Loren said, unsure if she should call Nancy Mommy or not. They hadn't talked about what happens if other people are in the house.

"Mommy?" The other woman knowingly suggested to Loren. Seeing Loren's eyes go wide and her head spin, Nancy smiled and walked over to her. Kissing her deeply and cupping her chin, Nancy made Loren meet her eyes and raised an eyebrow expectantly.

"Mommy," Loren half whispered, her voice suddenly hoarse.

"Sweetheart, this is Steff. We have been friends for years. She has a baby boy who is a bit older than you," Nancy said as Loren's neck caught her attention. She looked into Loren's eyes, and their broken stare was all she needed to know.

"It wasn't my fault, Mommy. I said no, nothing happened. I even quit my job. I'm never going back there. I never want that to happen again," Loren said as Nancy listened, Steff coming over to where they stood, curiosity on her face. Nancy looked furious, making Loren unnerved and tears well up in her eyes.

"Tell me what happened baby," Nancy said sternly making Loren confused, unsure of where Nancy's anger would be directed. Loren explained what had happened, looking from Nancy to Steff. Steff took Loren's hands in hers, but Nancy was not so expressive. She just sat there, listening to Loren's story as rage boiled inside of her. *How fucking dare they*, she said to herself as Loren told her how the man had choked her, his markings still clearly imprinted on her neck. As Loren finished the story, she looked nervously at Nancy. Then to Steff who gave Nancy a look, Loren didn't know the meaning of.

"I hope you're not mad and don't mind I quit Mommy, I just really don't want to go back there," Loren added for the fifth time, worried Nancy would be mad she had made such a rash decision.

"I'm not mad at you at all. I'm mad at them. I'm more than mad; I'm livid. I don't care if they buy the house or not, we are going to the police," Nancy said as she scooped up Loren and held her tightly, rocking her in her arms.

"But they'll just say I had a history; it'll get out that this was something I did. They'll say it's my fault. It'll get twisted," Loren replied as tears rolled down her cheeks for the fourth time that day.

"I don't want to have to relive it, Mommy," Loren said through her tears. Steff understood what Nancy had told her about Loren at that moment. Over lunch, Nancy had explained how fragile Loren was, how untrained and independent she was. How she would make decisions for herself and not be simply led.

"I'm glad you quit. The money wasn't worth it. We can talk about going to the police later. Right now, do you need Mommy, or do you need to go for a run?" Nancy asked, wanting to make sure to give Loren what she needed. Loren turned to Steff who smiled, almost reading her mind.

"You haven't ruined anything, sweetheart," she kindly stated. Looking back at Nancy, Loren began to suck her thumb and reached out for Nancy.

"I want you, Mommy," she replied, feeling Nancy tighten her arms around her. Nancy put Loren on her lap and turned her around to face Steff.

"She's adorable Nance," she said, wishing her baby boy was in her arms.

"She's a good girl," Nancy replied, smiling like the cat who got the cream.

"Steff is going to stay the night baby. Maybe Phil wants to come over for a play?" Nancy asked.

"Phil wants whatever I tell him he wants. He will be here in an hour," Steff laughed as she took out her phone while stroking Loren's cheek making her giggle. Steff was sterner than Nancy. She had an angular face and eyes that meant business. Loren wondered if it was because she had a boy baby and not a girl, making a mental note to not get on Steff's angry side.

"Let's get you out of this princess," Nancy said as she carried Loren into the nursery. Nancy laid Loren on her back on the pink mat, and Steff played with her on the floor while Nancy took out the things she needed.

"You know, we have never had a play date," Steff said as Loren reached for the toy she was holding high in the air.

"I know. That's because I've never had such a sweet girl," Nancy said as she came over to where Loren was playing and picked her up, carrying her to the changing table. Loren obediently lifted her bottom and let Nancy take her shorts off. She blushed as Steff came close and put a pacifier into her mouth and Nancy noted Loren was pushing through her comfort zone to let another person see her like this.

"She's a good girl for Mommy," Nancy said to Steff as Loren began to squirm, settling her with a warning in her voice. Nancy powdered Loren's pussy and added another layer to her diaper, making it thicker than the one she had on the previous night. She tightened it in place before holding up two choices of diaper cover for Loren to choose from.

"Oh wow, she had you wrapped around her finger!" Steff exclaimed upon witnessing Nancy, allowing Loren to choose what she would wear.

"She knows that if she isn't good, this will be taken away. Mommy doesn't mind treating her princess, but if she thinks she can be bratty afterward, all Mommy's treats go," Nancy said, putting on the tight fluffy leopard print diaper cover. She looked into Loren's eyes lovingly as she rubbed the diaper against Loren's pussy firmly making her giggle.

"Does it feel nice pushing against your pussy baby," Nancy said as she looked down on Loren.

"Yes, Mommy," Loren replied with her pacifier still in her mouth.

"Oh she's cute," Steff said as she ran her hands over her diapered sides through the fluffy material making Loren squirm as she felt another person touch her. Nancy watched as Loren's confused face went from Steff to her, wondering if it was OK to let Steff touch her. Nancy smiled and turned back towards the cupboard and took out a tight white t-shirt. After taking Loren's orange singlet off, Nancy pulled the t-shirt on and grabbed a pair of knee-high black socks.

"There baby," Nancy said as she took a pink blanket and wrapped it around Loren. Nancy carried Loren back out to the living room and put her on the couch. Steff tickled Loren as she rolled on her socks while Nancy fed her a bottle.

"No you can't have these right now sweetheart, they are for night nights," Nancy loving stated when Loren pushed her bottle away and reached for Nancy's massive breasts as a knock came from the door. Steff jumped up to get it, excited her little prince was here.

"Hi, baby boy. I have a new friend for you to play with," Steff said, taking the bag the man was carrying, holding his hand and walking him into the living room. Loren shifted uncomfortably in Nancy's arms as she began to blush.

"Hi Nancy," the man said in a small voice.

"Hello Phil, have you been a good boy for Steff?" Nancy replied, rocking Loren.

"Yes, Nancy," he answered, looking at Loren.

"This is Loren Phil; she's Nancy's baby girl. You'll have to play gently with her; she's not as big as you," Steff said as Phil got on his knees and crawled over to where Nancy was holding Loren. Phil reached in to touch Loren's hand, and Nancy wondered what would happen. *Either she'll pull away, or she'll be excited to play with him*, she thought to herself, smiling at Loren and Steff when Loren pushed off Nancy's soft stomach to touch Phil's nose. Squirming to get down to the ground, Nancy carried Loren to the middle of the large living room and watched as Phil showed her his toys. Loren spent her time, biting all of them as he passed her one after another.

"This is crazy, she had made so much progress," Nancy said as she and Steff watched their babies play from the kitchen.

"Yeah, I don't think I would have handled her as well as you have. I love how dependent he is on me. I find it hard giving him his one a week of complete independence," Steff replied praising Nancy.

"I have known her for five years, though. I already knew who she was when she's Loren. Who she is, is just amplified when she's in her little space. I already knew she was fragile and a runner. I already knew she wouldn't respond to an overly firm hand. And I only give her a choice because I want to know the type of thing she likes. She's got a cool style I must admit. I want her to be more dependent on me sure, but that's a process, and I'm quite impressed at the progress we've made so far! I mean look at her, she couldn't even look at me when she first saw the nursery, and now she's openly diapered and playing in her little space. This is huge," Nancy replied as Steff passed her wine, and they made their way back to the living room. Phil had begun to draw a picture of his toys, and he gave a crayon to Loren who started scribbling on the piece of paper he put down for her.

"Has she wet her diaper yet?" Steff asked as she took off Phil's shoes. Making Loren's head snap around and look at Nancy.

"Not yet," Nancy said in a voice that made it very clear it would be something which was going to happen.

Chapter 7

Steff and Phil had stayed in one of Nancy's spare rooms that evening. After hours of playing of giggling, Phil and Loren had fallen asleep watching a movie and Nancy had gently picked Loren up and brought her into the nursery, placing her in the cot. As Loren woke in the morning, she panicked searching for Nancy, who was nowhere to be found. Realizing she was in the cot, Loren climbed out and slowly walked out of the room where she heard Phil's voice.

"Hi Loren," he excitedly said upon seeing her watch him. Loren shyly smiled as she watched him play with a train set.

"Wanna play?" Phil was still in his train pajamas, and Loren made a note that he loved trains. Nodding, she dropped to her knees and crawled over to him. Phil gave Loren a train and moved her hand over it on the train tracks, showing her how to play. Giggling, Loren bent over the train set and pushed the train around the tracks. Phil watched her.

"You're good at that Loren," he said still in his little space.

"Thanks," she replied as Nancy walked up to them.

"Oh hello there miss," Nancy said as Loren reached up for her. Bending down, Nancy picked her up, and Loren giggled as Nancy kissed her cheeks.

"I escaped Mommy," Loren said proudly.

"I can see that baby girl. Are you playing with Phil's trains?" Nancy asked, putting her back down on the ground and roughing up Phil's hair.

"Yes Mommy, Phil showed me how to do this," Loren said as she moved a train around the tracks.

"That's my boy, always trying to impress the pretty girls," Steff said, coming around the corner.

"Morning," Nancy said as she turned on the coffee machine.

"Phil, did you forget what day it is today?" Steff asked as she began to put the trains away. He thought for a minute before looking embarrassed, he forgot.

"It's my big boy day Steff," he said excitedly. Loren looked at Nancy for an explanation, but she was busy in the kitchen.

"What's a big boy day Steff?" Loren asked curiously.

"Every Saturday, Phil gets to do all the things the big boys do. He can do whatever he wants and doesn't have to ask me for anything," Steff said taking the trains Loren was handing to her. Loren crawled towards the kitchen and waited for Nancy like she had been told to do.

"Let me guess," Nancy said knowingly as she looked into Loren's overly excited eyes.

"My baby girl wants a big girl day too?" Nancy continued, walking past Loren and handing Steff a coffee.

"Yes, please Mommy," Loren eagerly replied, following her back into the living room.

"Well, I don't see why that couldn't work. But look at you baby, I don't think you look like a big girl at all," Nancy stated as Phil walked back into the room. Loren hadn't noticed his broad back and muscular arms before, but as he strutted into the living room in well-fitting jeans, a designer polo and smelling of expensive cologne with all confidence in the world, she saw a completely different side to him.

"What do you guys have planned today?" He asked in a deep voice, making Loren's eyes wide with amusement; it was very different from his baby boy voice. Steff looked playfully annoyed at his bravado as he opened a red bull.

"Nice breakfast," she commented. While Steff and Phil spoke, Loren had crawled to the couch and climbed into Nancy's lap, hugging her tightly and sucking her thumb.

"Please, Mommy, I'll do anything you want," Loren begged.

"That is the most dangerous sentence you could have used my sweet girl. I'll hold you to that," Nancy said as she rubbed Loren's pussy through her fluffy pants and diapered pussy. Steff smiled at Nancy knowingly and went back to talking to Phil.

"I don't know what you guys are going to do, but I'm going to find out just how badly my baby girl wants to have a grown up day," Nancy said as she took Loren's hand and led her into the nursery.

"Lay down sweetheart," Nancy said lovingly as she snapped her fingers to the pink rug in the middle of the room. Loren obediently followed hoping that whatever Nancy had planned it would go fast. Her mind was racing with all the things she could spend her day doing.

"You only have to do one thing for me," Nancy began to say making Loren smile.

"Wet your diaper," she continued, watching Loren's smile turn into shock.

"But Mommy, I know we talked about it, but we didn't say when," Loren began to complain as Nancy took a pacifier and stuck it into Loren's mouth. As Loren reached up to take it out, Nancy turned around swiftly as if knowing Loren would try to protest further.

"Don't you dare," she commanded in a voice that made Loren drop her hand and shift uncomfortably.

"This is what I want. You said you'd do anything I wanted. This is it baby girl. The faster you wet your diaper, the faster you can go out and do all the big girl things you want," Nancy explained.

"I don't have to tell you that if you don't give me what I want and waste my time you won't enjoy the outcome do I, sweetheart?" Nancy asked as she pushed Loren back, making her lay down on the floor and stood over her. Loren shook her head no and began to squirm as Nancy pressed her foot onto her stomach.

"I know you haven't been to the bathroom since last night princess. I don't fight Mommy. I'll always win," Nancy continued as Loren fought not to wet her diaper although she desperately needed to. Loren held up her arms to Nancy, wanting to be cuddled.

"Oh I think the baby is trying to control Mommy," Nancy said, taking Loren's hands and slapping them, making her bring them back to her chest. Nancy bent down next to Loren and ran her fingers through Loren's messy ponytail.

"Are you nervous baby? You want Mommy to cuddle you and make you feel safe while you wet your diaper?" Nancy teased as Loren nodded her head, her eyes beginning to well. Nancy had never been so lenient with a girl before. She would have usually tied a girl to the cot and kept her there until she had wet her diaper, but Loren was different. It wasn't that she was naughty, and Nancy knew she wasn't trying to control the situation. It was that she needed more love than any girl Nancy ever had before. Most new situations scared her regardless of how much she wanted or liked it. This was no different. Nancy sat down and patted her lap and enjoying seeing Loren eagerly crawl into her arms.

"Good girl," Nancy cooed as she rubbed Loren through her

diaper. Kissing the top of her head and rocking her gently.

"Wet your diaper for Mommy baby," she continued as she kept on hand on the front of Loren's diaper, feeling her relax and begin to push against the hand Nancy was using to groped her.

"Mommy," Loren said softly as she turned her head and breathed into Nancy's ample cleavage. Nancy smiled triumphantly as she felt Loren's diaper become warm in her hand.

"Good girl baby," Nancy continued as Loren's face went red and her head bent in shame. Nancy kissed Loren's cheeks, and the top of her head as Loren continued to wet her diaper.

"Doesn't that feel better baby girl?" Nancy asked as Loren reached for her bunny.

"Yes, Mommy," Loren replied as she was handed bunny by Nancy. Loren looked down and tried to move away from her wet diaper, not enjoying the feeling of being dirty.

"You want it off, baby?" Nancy said, enjoying Loren's apparent discomfort.

"Yes please, Mommy," Loren forced herself to say loudly although wanting to whisper. She didn't want to give Nancy any reason to keep it on any longer.

"Lucky I'm such a nice Mommy then isn't it baby?" Nancy asked as she laid Loren on her back and began to take off the wet diaper. After wiping her down, Nancy left her on the floor to dry while she went to her room and chose panties for Loren to wear.

Loren clapped her hands excitedly as she saw what Nancy was carrying as she came back into the room. Nancy stood over the top of Loren once again, shooting fear through Loren that something else would happen.

"Take that off," Nancy commanded, pointing to her t-shirt, Loren quickly followed Nancy's instructions and passed the shirt to her receiving her panties in exchange.

"Well, don't you want them on? I can easy diaper you again if you'd like to go out wearing your baby clothes?" Nancy mocked, making Loren laugh as she put on her panties.

"So," Loren said hesitantly, unsure of what do now.

"So? So now you can do whatever you want," Nancy replied as she watched Loren. Standing up, Loren walked over to Nancy and looked her up and down.

"Can we talk about how this is all going?" Loren asked. Nancy laughed and nodded, shutting the door to the nursery behind Loren and following her into her room. Nancy walked to her room and sat on the bed, watching as Loren got dress.

"So like, you're my Mommy, and I call you Mommy when we are in the house regardless of what space I'm in and who is here, I've got that," Loren stated to speak, looking at Nancy for confirmation. Nancy nodded her head and watched as Loren continued.

"But on Saturday's I can have a day where I do whatever I want. And during the day I am a big girl, but after the day is done, I'm your baby. Are you like my girlfriend on Saturday and during the day?" Loren asked, sitting down next to Nancy after she pulled on her ripped jeans and her favorite old band, singlet.

"OK. So, yeah you can refer to me as your girlfriend for convince sake if people ask you about me, you know, like friends or whoever. But I'm your Mommy, not your fucking girlfriend and there's a big power difference in those titles which I don't want you to get confused. Like we've said previously, this is a non-negotiable monogamous dynamic. It would be cheating if you were to be with someone else even on Saturday's. I can be your "girlfriend" as in we can do fancy dinners and romantic things together. You can get dressed in the most beautiful outfits, and I'd love to take out and paint the town, but I am your Mommy. So if we go to the movies for example and I say you've had enough candy or whatever and you don't either give me the bag or you just ignore me, that's still punishable. You're not just my baby when you're in diapers sucking on my milky tits; you're my baby full time, the rules we have don't change, only your headspace and outward expression changes," Nancy explained.

"Oh OK, that makes so much sense. So if I found a job and was like, 'Can we go out to this event', or something after work spontaneously, you'd either say yes or no, and then we'd go and if you said that I'd had enough beer for example and I keep drinking, I'd be in trouble," Loren said confirming with Nancy.

"You got it. Don't get me wrong; I'm not interested in

locking you up every night. I want to do fun things. Still, I'm so happy you're finally mine but when we get home from doing whatever you're my little girl, and I'll treat you that way," Nancy said pulling Loren in and kissing her deeply.

"This is the best thing I've ever done," Loren said as she broke the kiss.

"I know," Nancy replied, reaching into Loren's pants and biting her bottom lip feeling how wet Loren was.

Chapter 8

Nancy and Loren slowly developed their lifestyle, going to gallery openings and bespoke bars. They blew cash on expensive shopping trips and ate out at the best restaurants. They added toys and clothes to the nursery, and Loren found a new job that paid less but was fewer hands-on experiences. Loren loved the way Nancy took the time to teach her what she wanted instead of punishing her for things she didn't know. After the three months, they had spent together, Loren had a handle on everything Nancy expected of her. Nancy had specifically told Loren that she would begin punishing her for forgetting a rule, and they had bought the paddle Nancy would use to hand out the punishment.

On a sunny Saturday, Loren had decided to go out with her old boss Jen, day drinking and shopping, throwing money around a casino and dancing with strangers to the street bands playing down alleys.

"I've been so worried about you," Jen said as Loren broke away from dancing and walked back out onto the main street.

"Why?" Loren asked in a drunken haze.

"Um, hello? You just up and leave one day over the phone and I don't hear from you for like two months, and now we meet up, and you're the happiest I've ever seen you!" Jen explained.

"Hmm," Loren sighed contently.

"It's Nancy. She's amazing," she added as they walked towards the subway.

"Café Nancy? Like, significantly older than you Nancy?" Jen asked, surprisingly.

"That'd be the one," Loren replied lovingly.

"OK, wait like you guys are fucking or dating or what?" Jen questioned, confused as to what Loren was talking about.

"Jen. I'm with Nancy, we fuck, we go on dates, we do a whole lot of what and it's awesome," Loren said wanting to end the conversation.

"Right, well I'm just surprised," Jen said defensively.

"That's fine, be surprised, turns out I'm very surprising," Loren teased as she hugged Jen goodbye and entered the subway, heading back home. Loren pulled on her headphones and was whisked away into a world of carefree bliss, almost skipping her way home.

Opening the door to Nancy's apartment, Loren dropped her bag at the door and connected her phone to the Bluetooth speakers, pumping music through the house. It was 5:30 in the afternoon, and after ordering a pizza and opening a beer, Loren danced around the living room until her pizza arrived. She heard a knock at the door, tipped the pizza boy more generously that required, and slammed the door behind him. Taking a slice, folding it in half and moaning in appreciation, Loren made her way to the kitchen and flicked through social media on her phone. In her heightened state of bliss and drunken haze, Loren didn't hear the front door open, and Nancy walk in. *What the actual fuck Loren*, Nancy playfully thought as she saw Loren at the kitchen bench dancing in her seat. Seeing the shopping bags at the door, the pizza box and beer bottles on the kitchen table, Nancy smiled, happy Loren was enjoying her day.

"Hi baby," Nancy whispered startling Loren who jumped. She turned the music off and turned around, shocked to see what Nancy wearing. A low-cut almost see through light blue blouse which exposed the front of her breasts and dark denim jeans which held to her curves.

"Damn, Nancy. You look amazing," Loren slightly slurred, her eyes glazing over making Nancy tilt her head.

"Mm, what did you just say?" Nancy asked, wondering if Loren in her drunken state would warrant forgiveness. Deciding she most definitely wouldn't let Loren off the hook, Nancy tried to suppress an excited knowing smile.

"I said you looked amazing," Loren said, unaware of how much trouble she was in.

"I heard that. But I didn't hear Mommy, what did I hear instead?" Nancy questioned, raising an eyebrow in satisfaction as Loren's grew full with the awareness of what she had said.

"Well?" Nancy stated.

"I um, called you Nancy," Loren said, sobering up very quickly.

"Yeah, you did baby. What was my rule on that?" Nancy asked, drinking Loren's beer.

"Not too," Loren said, realizing she was fucked.

"Yeah, so guess what sweetheart, Mommy's going to punishment for not following my straightforward rule," Nancy said as she finished the beer and slammed it down on the bench making Loren jump.

"Good, be scared baby. That would be wise," Nancy said as an evil smile spread across her face. Grabbing Loren's hair, she pulled hard, making her stumble to her feet and wince in pain as she was towed to the nursery. Nancy didn't speak as she pushed Loren against the wall and cuffed her wrists in place. She went to the changing table drawer and took out a pair of scissors and walked over to a scared Loren.

"No Mommy," Loren begged, fear escaping her voice.

"No, Mommy? Oh, I'm Mommy again? Funny about that," Nancy said, ignoring Loren's fear. As she roughly pulled on Loren's shirt and began to cut it off. She cut off her bra next and violently threw the material to the other side of the room.

"I'm sorry, Mommy," Loren begged.

"Oh, you have no idea how sorry you're going to be little one. What's my name, baby?" Nancy asked as she undid Loren's denim shorts. *These are too cute to cut*; she thought as she wriggled them down Loren's thighs.

"Mommy," Loren said, pulling away from Nancy who was cupping her pussy.

"That's right baby," Nancy said as she began to rub Loren's pussy, firmly squeezing her making her pull away again.

"I thought I taught you better than to pull away from me baby," Nancy said as she cut off Loren's panties.

"Stick it out for me," Nancy said while walking to the cupboard. Loren obeyed and swallowed hard when she saw what Nancy was holding in her hand.

"Oh, baby, you look scared. Are you scared of what Mommy is going to do to you?" Nancy teased as she pushed a pacifier into Loren's mouth and covered it in tape.

"I don't want to hear you," Nancy said as she pinched Loren's nipples until she heard a muffled cry of pain.

"You should be scared, little girl. You've made Mommy very angry, and I'm going to take it out on your pussy," Nancy whispered in Loren's ear as she pulled hard on her nipple. Whack. Nancy struck Loren's pussy with a paddle making her gasp in pain and double over.

"I wouldn't move if I were you, baby," Nancy said as she readied her paddle.

"Wider," Nancy commanded, pressing Loren against the wall with her other hand. Whack, whack, whack. Loren began to whimper but held in place.

"Good girl. That was for pulling away from me. You made yourself get double the punishment, wasn't that silly baby," Nancy said as she paddled Loren's pussy three more times, each time hearing Loren whimper louder than the last. Her pussy began to get tender and swollen, and Nancy rubbed it with her warm hands as she spoke to Loren.

"What's my name, baby?" She asked, trying to catch Loren's eye.

"Mommy," Loren said through her gag as she looked down, a tear falling to the floor.

"Look at me baby," Nancy gruffly ordered as she wiped Loren's tears away.

"What is it?" She pressed.

"Mommy," Loren repeated, looking Nancy in the eye. Nancy smiled, whack, whack, whack, whack, whack, and stopped once Loren's legs gave way, and she fell. Getting to her feet as quickly as she could Loren spoke as tears ran down her face.

"Crying will get you, nothing, sweetheart. I know you want this to stop, but it doesn't matter what you want. You're Mommy's baby girl and you'll be punished until I'm satisfied," Nancy said as she pinched Loren's nipples.

"I don't want this anymore," Nancy said as she put away the paddle and took out a butt plug and lubed it slowly in front of Loren.

"This will look so pretty baby," Nancy said as she poked

Loren's arsehole with it, pushing it in while Loren winced in pain.

"Why are you fighting it? I told you, Mommy, always wins," Nancy said, laughing as she forced it inside of Loren and began to finger fuck tender pussy.

"I'm going to force you to cum baby. I know you're not wet, I don't you don't feel horny, but you're my baby, and when I want you to cum, you'll bloody well cum," Nancy said as she continued to force two fingers inside Loren's tight and ever increasingly wet pussy. As Loren began to moan and grind down on Nancy's fingers, only causing Nancy to use her harder.

"That didn't take long," Nancy stated as Loren covered her hand suddenly. She took her fingers out of Loren's aching pussy and wiped her juices over her stomach, drying off her hand. Nancy un-cuffed Loren's wrists and ripped the tape off her mouth, making her eyes water. Loren's legs buckled underneath her and Nancy lovingly carried to the changing table and rubbed soothing cream over Loren's red pussy. She cleaned Loren's stomach and sprinkled the powder on her so that she wouldn't chaff and put her in a diaper. She picked a light grey onesie with matching with light pink knee-high socks. After Nancy put Loren's hair in a messy ponytail, she placed a light pink bowed headband in her hair and gave her a pacifier, her blankie, and bunny and carried her to the living room. Cradling Loren in one arm, she undid the blouse which had caused all Loren's problems and began to nurse her.

"Good girl baby," Nancy cooed as she rocked Loren while she nursed.

"You've been such a good girl for Mommy, taking your punishment. I don't like having to punish you, sweetie. But we have rules, and they will be followed," Nancy explained. Loren nodded as warm milk flowed into her mouth. Nancy placed her large hand on Loren's tummy and gently patted her.

"You're not going to forget Mommy's name again, will you?" Nancy asked, already knowing the answer. Loren took Nancy's nipple out of her mouth, and milk ran down her cheek.

"No Mommy," she replied quickly before Nancy filled her mouth once again, cleaning the side of her face with her blankie. Smiling, Nancy held onto Loren and watched as she rested in her arms.

Chapter 9

A month later the café had been booked out for a function that night, and Nancy would be staying late, and Steff had offered to have Loren over, so she wasn't alone. Loren had initially told Nancy that one night without her wouldn't be a problem, but she liked that Nancy had ignored her. Nancy, Steff, and Loren had come up with an agreement for what was OK and for what was simply not. Steff could put Loren in a diaper when she got there, bottle-feed her, kiss her cheek and cuddle her but anything sexual was strictly off the table. Loren would sleep in Steff's bedroom if she felt tired instead of Phil's and would take her toys. She would feed herself anything but her bottle and would use the bathroom if she needed to go. Steff had some rules that Loren had to follow, like waiting until she had finished eating dinner before Phil or Loren could have theirs. Staying on the floor, not the couch and strictly crawling on the carpeted surfaces. Any rule breaking or complaining would result in a firm bare arse spanking Steff assured Loren would not stop until she was crying uncontrollably.

"She's a quick crier Steff. If she's naughty, let's wait until Mommy is there, so I can watch her be spanked, so disappointed in you after Steff has been so good to have you," Nancy said as

Loren looked at both of them nervously.

"I won't break your rules, Steff," Loren said reassuringly. Steff smiled kindly, half hoping she would.

"You'll be punished even if you break them by accident, OK sweetheart?" Steff more stated than asked a nodding Loren.

"Good, we'll see you then," she had added as she left Nancy's apartment. The day had arrived where Loren would go to Steff's after work.

"So baby tell Mommy again what the plan is," Nancy said as she cut up Loren's breakfast.

"I'm going straight to Steff's after work and staying there until you pick me up. Maybe you'll be late, and I go to sleep there. Steff is in charge, and I can trust her to be nice," Loren said by heart before she ate a mouthful of bacon and egg.

"Good girl," Nancy said.

"I'm serious about not breaking her rules. She's a lot meaner than Mommy is. You won't like her punishment, and she won't stop just because I'm there, you know what you agreed to," Nancy warned, worried Loren might try to test Steff's boundaries.

"I won't be naughty Mommy, I promise. I don't want her to punish me. Phil told me not to mess with her either. He said she put a vibrator in his arse and kept his cock locked for a whole weekend once," Loren replied knowingly. Nancy lowered the spoon, shocked at the words Loren was using.

"Baby, Mommy doesn't like you using such foul language. Don't speak like that again, alright?" Nancy said in a loving but deadly-serious voice. Loren blushed, she knew that if she spoke like that again, she would be punished, and she hated being punished.

"Sorry Mommy, I won't," Loren said as she ate her last mouthful. Loren finished getting ready, kissed Nancy goodbye, and headed to work.

For anyone looking at her, Loren would have appeared to be a typically beautiful woman with possessions worth envying and a devil may care attitude that had people falling for her without her trying.

As she finished work and headed to the subway to Steff's house, she looked longing into her bag as she saw her bunny and pacifier. Jointed out of her train of thought, she felt the knee of a fancy business-suited man.

"Mind if I sit?" The man asked. Loren looked up annoyed, but her annoyance quickly fading when she realized who was standing in front of her.

"Phil?" Loren asked with a smile.

"Hi," he replied, nodding to her bag.

"Excited?" Phil asked.

"Nervous," Loren answered. She looked at his debonair

appearance and wondered how he and Steff had met.

"Don't be, just," he cut himself off and looked around the carriage. Leaning in, he whispered in her ear, "Just be a good girl for Steff, and she'll love you." Loren leaned back blushing. Phil had used his little voice, and he giggled slightly and looked down bashfully. Clearing his throat, he readjusted his shoulders and gained the all-powerful glare he wore so well, making Loren laugh.

"Don't even pretend," she said as he grinned at her. Stepping out of the subway, Phil led her to Steff's.

"Why do you call her Steff?" Loren asked while they walked down a quiet street.

"The same reason you call Nancy, Mommy," Phil replied, whispering the word Mommy.

"I was told to," he added, looking at his watch.

"Don't you ever want to call her something more, I don't know, Mommy like?" Loren asked unsatisfied with his answer.

"Not really. We've been together for six years; she's Steff to me. I guess she's a different version of Steff to me than other people, but it's never really crossed my mind to question it," Phil replied honestly.

"Wow, six years," Loren stated in awe. She and Nancy had only been together for just over six months.

"Yeah, it goes fast!" Phil said as he pointed to a house in a leafy suburban street.

"We're here," he added, checking the mailbox and walking up the front path. Loren wasn't lying when she said she was nervous. She began to wonder if this was the best idea to have agreed to come here. It was new and therefore, scary.

"Hi guys," Steff said, opening the door before Phil could find the keys. She stepped aside and let them in. Loren looking for carpet, stood in the entrance way until Steff took her hand and pulled her indoors, shutting and locking the door behind her.

"Phil, I expect you to do what you know you need to do while I settle Loren in," she said in her no-nonsense manner. Phil nodded and walking up the wooden hallway, turned into a room and disappeared. Steff took Loren's hand and bag off her shoulder and led her to a room on the other side of the house.

"Kneel," Steff commanded clicking her fingers to the floor. Loren obediently knelt, as Steff put her bag on her bed and took out Loren's shower gel, tooth-brush, and pajamas, diaper and pacifier.

"Come with me," Steff said, holding out her hand to Loren who took it and stood back up. Steff took her into the bathroom and ran a bath.

"You're a very quiet girl, sweet pea. Are you nervous?" Steff asked as she began to undress Loren, running her hands over her body, enjoying how smooth her skin felt.

"Yes, Steff," Loren answered as she began to suck her

thumb. Steff shook her head and took Loren's thumb out of her mouth.

"You're not clean yet baby, here," Steff said, putting the pacifier into Loren's mouth. Steff held Loren's hand as she helped her into the bath. Loren loved the bubbles Steff had put in the tub and played as Steff ran warm water over her body and washed her clean.

"There," Steff said when she was satisfied. She held out a towel and dried Loren, cuddling her and making her giggle. Steff laid Loren down on the towel in the bathroom and put on her diaper.

"These are cute," Steff said as she held up the diaper cover Nancy had chosen for Loren, a thick, white fluffy material cover with pink rabbits printed on it. Steff put the cover over Loren's diaper and rubbed her hands over her thickly padded bottom.

"Oh, doesn't that feel good little girl," she said lovingly. Taking a light pink long sleeve, Steff gently pulled it over Loren's head and continued to dress her, adding matching grey knee-high socks.

"You're the sweetest," Steff admired as she looked at the baby girl she had before her. Leaving Loren's hair in her signature messy ponytail, Steff led Loren back to her room.

"Do you want your toys, baby?" Steff asked nicer than Loren was prepared for. Nodding yes, Loren took out her paci and replied, "Yes, please Steff."

"Then crawl to me," Steff replied, eyeing Loren in a way that made her nervous. Loren began to crawl to Steff who handed her her bunny. Steff ran her fingers over Loren's head and smiled when Loren cuddled her legs.

"Come on, baby, let's see what Phil is doing," she said to Loren, who followed her back out into the living room where Phil was already playing.

"I drew a picture," he told Loren as he held it up for her to see. Loren smiled behind her paci as Steff looked over from the kitchen.

"Don't let her have the crayons, Phil, I need to give her a bottle, and I don't want her hands covered in crayon," she called. Loren sat down and remembering she wasn't allowed on the couch; she waited as she watched Phil do another drawing.

"It's a fire truck," Phil explain coloring it in red. Steff came out from behind the kitchen bench and sat on the couch, patting her lap while looking at Loren.

"Come here," she said in a stern voice. Loren quickly crawled to her feet where Steff picked her up and cradled her in her arms. Steff was slender, and her thin arms were boney. Loren squirmed uncomfortably, missing Nancy's more full and thick-set curvy body.

"Stop fussing," Steff plainly said as she gently slapped Loren's upper thigh making her stop. Steff took Loren's hands and held them down as she took out her paci and pushed the rubber nipple of the bottle into her mouth. Loren instinctively began to drink the warmed milk in her bottle, and Steff relaxed back on the couch. Phil looked up at Steff, who smiled back at him.

"You don't need a bottle; you're a big boy. Loren is a baby," she stated as if reading his mind.

"But Steff," Phil began to complain only to be summoned to Steff's feet.

"Kneel," Steff commanded waiting until Phil was in front of her before backhanding him across the face making Loren nervous.

"When did I say you could talk back to me?" Steff said, half yelled.

"Never Steff," Phil said, looking down, trying to hide his anger.

"Don't start with me, boy. I will not have you play up just because Loren is here. You should be showing her how well-behaved you are not a naughty boy for me," Steff said as she rubbed his red cheek affectionately. After Loren finished her bottle, Steff put her back down on the floor and went to order dinner leaving Phil and Loren alone.

"Do you want to play wrestling?" Phil asked. Loren shook her head no.

"You're no fun," he said bitterly making Loren look around uncomfortably.

"Do you want to play with bunny?" Loren asked hopefully handing Phil her bunny. Phil looked at it and threw it down the hallway.

"No," he said, making Loren frown and pout. Loren began to crawl down the hallway to collect her bunny when she saw Steff coming out of her bedroom, hanging up the phone.

"How did this get here?" She asked Loren playfully. Loren looked back at Phil and pointed.

"He didn't want to play with bunny, so he threw her away," Loren said as she cuddled bunny.

"Oh I think somebody is a little jealous they have to share," Steff said, walking into that living room.

"I am not," Phil spat out as he scrunched up his drawing and threw it at the wall. Steff lifted her white pullover revealing a big silver belt buckle and brown leather belt.

"Oh boy I'm not even going to ask you to try that again, get over here," Steff said, aggressively making Loren's mouth gaped open. Unbuckling her belt, Steff removed it in one sweeping motion. Loren watched as Steff ripped down Phil's flannel, train-print pajama pants and pulled him onto her lap. Striking him without warning, Phil cried out, making Loren uncomfortable. Steff continued to belt Phil's arse until it was so red that Loren thought for sure he would pass out from the pain any minute. Steff didn't speak a word for the whole time, but Phil made enough noise for the both of them. Howling and crying he stayed as still as he could as time after time Steff belted his arse raw.

"You can sit there and think about how you should be behaving," Steff said as she put Loren back on her lap and cuddled her in front of him making him pout and frown jealously. Loren buried her head into Steff's model like neck and tried to relax. Her heart was racing, and Steff felt it against her chest. Patting Loren on her back and rocking her soothingly Steff felt her begin to melt into her. Smiling wickedly at Phil, Steff snapped her fingers to her feet where Phil quickly crawled to.

"Are you going to be a good boy now, or do I need to belt your little arse again?" Steff asked, putting a calm Loren down on the floor.

"I'll be good; I'm sorry Steff," Phil replied as a knock came from the front door. Loren looked excitedly to the door, making Steff laugh.

"I don't think it's Mommy Loren," she said, getting up and going to the door, paying the delivery guy and coming back with her order. Steff laid the food out on the table and began eating as Phil and Loren drew pictures and played with his train set.

"Can bunny play?" Loren asked, hopefully. Phil looked at her and then looked at the bunny. Hearing Steff clear her throat he reluctantly agreed and put Loren's bunny on top of a train letting her push it around the tracks.

By 11:30, Loren had been put to bed by Steff. Steff watched as

Loren fell asleep admiring how sweet she was as she held her bunny and sucked her thumb. Phil and Steff began to watch a movie and Steff let Phil rest his head on her lap as she stroked him to sleep. At 1:30, a knock came from the door, and Steff carefully put Phil's head on the floor as she opened the door for Nancy.

"Hi, sorry it's so late," Nancy said as she came inside, greeting Steff in a warm embrace.

"How was your night?" Steff asked, shutting the door behind her.

"Long, my staff got put through the wringer. How was Loren?" Nancy asked as she looked around the living room for her.

"She was perfect; she's asleep. Phil got so jealous. He threw Loren's bunny up the hallway and back chatted me. I belted him in front of Loren; I think she'll be OK, I cuddled her afterward until she calmed down again. Easily scared. I think she was worried I'd spank her next," Steff said, offering Nancy a beer. Nancy laughed she had thought Phil would get jealous; she knew Loren would be jealous if her attention were on someone else.

"Yeah, she'll be fine. Oh! I needed that," Nancy said as she downed half the beer.

"Mommy?" Loren said as she sleepily rubbed her eyes, crawling out of Steff's room.

"Hi baby girl," Nancy said, turning around and walking

over to pick her up.

"Where you a good girl for Steff?" Nancy asked, holding Loren with one arm and drinking the rest of her beer. Loren looked at Steff and smiled sweetly.

"I think so," she replied. Nancy began to rub Loren's padded bottom, enjoying how soft and think it was and making a mental note to buy more diaper covers in this material.

"You think so?" Nancy teased, raising an eyebrow.

"Well, I didn't get spanked like Phil," Loren explained. Steff laughed as she walked over to Phil and pulled his pants down, revealing his still red arse. Nancy followed and chuckled when she saw.

"I'd hope you wouldn't need to be spanked like that. Should we try to see what happens?" Nancy asked, playfully.

"No, Mommy!" Loren replied, shocked that Nancy would suggest such a thing.

"Oh come on, it'll be fun to have Mommy spanking that pretty little bottom of yours," Nancy said, rubbing Loren's padded pussy, making her involuntarily push against her hand.

"I think you want it," Nancy whispered in Loren's ear. Putting Loren on the floor, Nancy pulled down the cover and undid her diaper. Sitting her up, Steff moved behind her and Nancy pushed Loren back against Steff.

"Let's see how excited you are," Nancy said as she put a finger in Loren's mouth making her suck it before sliding it up and down her pussy slit. Pushing through her lips, Loren bucked her hips, wanting Nancy inside of her.

"Mommy hasn't fucked you in weeks, isn't that right baby?" Nancy asked. Steff stroked Loren's hair and kissed her cheek as a wave of pleasure rolled over Loren making her breathless.

"Yes, Mommy," Loren said as she closed her eyes and bit her lip. Nancy played with Loren's clit and slid one finger into her tight wet pussy, making her moan loudly, waking Phil up. He looked around and was shocked to find Steff holding Loren in place while Nancy slowly fucked her.

"Stay," Steff commanded, clicking her fingers when she saw Phil wake up. She smiled as she saw his cock becoming harder as he watched Loren.

"You can play little boy," Steff said, making Phil smile as he reached into his pants and began stroking his cock. Nancy took her finger out of Loren, scooped her up with one arm and flung her over her knee in a smooth motion. Spank, spank, spank. Nancy rubbed Loren's arse after each spanking just enough to keep her on the edge of her pain threshold.

"You'll be a good girl and take this baby. Mommy wants to see your arse go red," Nancy said as she pushed down on Loren's back while her other hand spanked Loren over and over.

"Mommy," Loren begged as she stopped squirming and took the spanking.

"That's right. Mommy is going to spank you a little longer tonight. You've been such a good girl. I'm spanking you because I want to, not because you've been bad," Nancy explained, picking up that Loren thought she was in trouble.

"Oh, baby, you're turning Mommy on. Let me spank you a few more times," Nancy said, enjoying letting her more sadistic side out. She had been waiting to be able to slightly brutalize Loren. As the sting of each spanking began to be too much for Loren, Nancy spat on her hand and rubbed Loren's pussy, circling her clit and continued to spank her. Nancy could feel Loren's heartbeat on her thigh and felt her pussy begin to drip cum; Nancy shoved two fingers into Loren's pussy, making her scream. As Loren was roughly fucked, Nancy continued to spank her, moving down to the tops of her thighs and squeezing her tightly after each hit. Loren came hard as her pussy gushed cum over Nancy's hand and fell limb over Nancy's leg, beginning to whimper. Nancy forced herself to stop just as her juices began to flow and cuddled Loren. Aware Loren had been pushed past her limit.

"It's over baby. Mommy has stopped. You did so well, sweetheart," Nancy said as she kissed Loren's tears away. Loren pushed Nancy back against the couch defiantly and pinned her there, pouting, frowning and panting.

"You're OK, sweetie. We just pushed to a new level. Mommy wouldn't hurt you, we just went further than we have before, but you're OK," Nancy said reassuringly, letting Loren have some control. Loren turned around to see Phil being pegged by Steff who was reaching around and jerking him off at the same time. Nancy pulled Loren back to her and held her hands behind her back, making Loren squirm with fear. Nancy let her hands go and smiled in relief as Loren wrapped them around her neck and snuggled into her cleavage. Nancy picked her up and took her to Steff's room to collect her things.

"Mommy, can I please have these," Loren said as she groped Nancy's full breasts. Nancy slowly unbuttoned her blouse and took off her bra, exposing her large nipples for Loren.

"Yes baby," Nancy replied as she positioned Loren for nursing, holding her breast to Loren's mouth and rubbing her nipple over her lips until she opened her mouth and began to nurse while they waited for Steff and Phil to finish.

Chapter 10

Loren's head was a mess. After the night at Steff's, nothing made sense. She had seen a side of Nancy she had never seen in the whole time she had known her. It had been like something had taken over her, and the Nancy she knew had gone for an hour. Loren knew she had been distant towards Nancy since that night, but she didn't know how to go back to the blissful vulnerability she had shown her before. *She just changed*, Loren thought to herself as she watched Nancy make waffles.

It was Saturday, and after their waffles, Loren had gone to the beach. Not particularly enjoying it, but wanting to be alone, moreover, wanting to be away from Nancy. *How can I even trust her? How will I know if she's going to change-up like that?* Loren thought as she enjoyed the warmth of the sun. Nancy had felt Loren's distance as well.

"Seeing her so ready for the taking made me wild," she said to Steff over the phone.

"Yeah, you did take her pretty hard. Was she able to walk after you slammed her pussy like that?" Steff replied as she used Phil as a footstool.

"Barely. Steff, I wanted to hurt her. I was getting off on it. That's only happened a handful of times, and it's never worked out afterward," Nancy explained as she paced back and forth in the living room.

"Maybe you're just crueler than you have allowed yourself to be. Maybe you need someone more masochistic than Loren," Steff replied.

"No, I don't think that's it. It just when I see Loren so sleepy and vulnerable just makes me want to use her until she is broken. I guess that's what everyone else sees in her as well. I'm happy I was able to stop, she's got such pull power," Nancy said before Loren walked through the door.

"I'll call you later, I have to go," she quickly added seeing Loren and hanging up the phone.

"Hi baby," Nancy said, walking over and embracing Loren.

"Hey Mommy," Loren replied absently as she stood still and let Nancy hold her. Breaking the embrace, Loren walked to the kitchen and made herself a coffee.

"You want?" Loren asked Nancy, who shook her head.

"Can we talk about this?" Nancy asked as Loren sat at the kitchen bench after a week of walking on egg-shells.

"Talk about what?" Loren replied, pretending everything was fine. Nancy lifted her hand to stroke Loren's hair, and Loren flinched defensively.

"Talk about that," Nancy stated, pointing out the distance between them. Loren looked into her coffee cup and wished she knew the words to say.

"You go first," she said. Nancy cracked her neck and sat down next to Loren.

"OK. Since that night, I can see it, I can feel it, you aren't giving your whole self to me, and it sucks," Nancy started. Loren looked at her and continued to listen.

"I guess I just enjoy a rougher side and if you don't then," Nancy said, cutting herself off.

"Then what?" Loren said aggressively, her eyes burning a hole into Nancy.

"You don't get just to walk away from this because I got scared, Mommy," Loren said, adding Mommy in the hope she would be forgiven for speaking so out of turn. Nancy smiled, looking down to the floor.

"Baby," Nancy began to say, stopping herself. Loren looked up at her expectantly.

"No, you know what it might be good for us to have that time apart," Loren said quietly.

"There's a work thing I need to go to, I'll be out of town for four nights next week," Loren said plainly.

"Why," Nancy replied, hurt that Loren wanted to be away from her.

"Because," Loren stated getting up and going to the living room.

"No," Nancy commanded as she followed Loren, "We have to speak about this," she added, sitting down next to Loren.

"Speak about what?!" Loren spat back at her.

"That I'm just your fucktoy like I was for everyone else?" Loren added with tears in her eyes. Shocked, Nancy reached her for, but Loren pushed her hand away.

"Don't touch me," Loren aggressively stated. Nancy could feel her heart being to break as she saw the girl she so dearly loved pulling away from her.

"You are not my fucktoy Loren!" Nancy exclaimed hurt that Loren thought so.

"Then why would you use me like that?" Loren said as she began to weep. Nancy looked at Loren who had brought her knees to her chest and cried into herself.

"I never said it was OK to have Steff hold me down; I never said it was OK to spank me while Phil jerked off watching. You were the one who said there wouldn't be anything sexual that night and it was bloody fucking sexual Nancy!" Loren practically yelled as she got up and stood over Nancy who remained on the couch. Nancy raised an eyebrow hearing Loren say her name with such venom.

"I don't give a fuck!" Loren stated reading Nancy's face, being very aware she was breaking multiple rules by talking in such a manner.

"I didn't realize I'd hurt you so much," Nancy said, deciding to hear what Loren was telling her instead of focusing on the rules she was breaking. Loren stopped pacing around the living room and looked at Nancy.

"You did," Loren replied, forgetting she was meant to be angry.

"How can I even trust you now? She added, misery escaping her voice. Loren sat down next to Nancy in silence.

"I don't trust you anymore," Loren quietly said after some time. She got up and walked to Nancy's bedroom and slammed the door shut. Nancy remained on the couch as tears began to well in her eyes.

Loren had packed her bags the night of the fight and had gone to stay at Jen's. The following morning she had boarded the plane and gone to the conference, without saying another word to Nancy. At the meeting, Loren heard from artist after artist talk about their works and their inspiration. In the evenings, she had stayed in alone. The people she was at the conference with had invited her out two nights in a row, but she had declined both times making excuses for her lack of partying interest. On the third day of the conference, an artist she had listened to an hour earlier spotted Loren during the lunch break.

"Mind if I sit?" the artist said, standing over the top of Loren who ate her lunch alone as an eight seater table.

"Oh, this table is full sorry," Loren replied, making a joke for the first time in four days. The artist laughed and sat next to her.

"Vanessa, right?" Loren asked inquisitively.

"Yeah, Loren?" Vanessa replied. Loren nodded her head.

"Where are you from?" Vanessa asked. Loren looked at her for the first time. She had crimson color hair and looked like a cover girl from a 90's magazine. She wore flowing, whimsical clothing, and Loren wondered why she had wanted to sit next to her when they were so very different.

"Look, you seem lovely, but I'm not into small talk. I'm not into any small talk right now," Loren replied apologetically.

"That's OK; we don't need to talk, I can feel you're hurting," Vanessa replied. Loren looked at her disbelievingly.

"You can feel I'm hurting?" She stated, almost mockingly. Vanessa just nodded to which Loren rolled her eyes, making Vanessa laugh out loud.

"You don't believe me?" Vanessa asked.

"I don't know what to believe," Loren muttered. Vanessa held out her hand to Loren, who looked at her puzzlingly.

"Give me your hand," Vanessa insisted. Loren sighed and placed her hand on top of Vanessa's, who held it gently.

"Well, someone broke your heart," Vanessa said knowingly.

"You could have just looked at my face and reached the same conclusion," Loren stated bluntly pulling her hand away.

"But at least this time you aren't using sex as a coping method," Vanessa retorted, piquing Loren's curiosity.

"See, not so dumb after all," Vanessa said in a matter of fact manner that made Loren laugh and relax.

"Fair enough," Loren submitted.

"What now?" She added, looking at Vanessa.

"Tell me what happened," Vanessa suggested.

"Nope," Loren replied quickly as she finished her lunch.

"Loren, other people can't see what I can, you can't-fool me, I know you aren't always a big girl," Vanessa whispered making Loren sit back and looked at her in shock and horror.

"Are you Nancy's friend?" Loren asked as fear escaped her voice.

"No, but as I said, I can feel things, and seeing things. What happened? Let me help you," Vanessa kindly replied.

"You can't help me," Loren stated sadly.

"Not if you don't let me," Vanessa replied. Loren looked around; they were the only people in the lunch room.

"There was a miss-interpretation of a contract, and now it all just feels too scary," Loren honestly explained.

"Maybe I'm just too dumb to understand what I'm doing, or maybe she just found a loophole, but I can't imagine she would knowingly hurt me. She stopped when she was mid-orgasm when I couldn't take anymore. I don't know how to place any of this," she added as she began to tear up. Vanessa closed her eyes and breathed in deeply.

"She didn't mean to hurt you. She thought you would

enjoy it and when she realized she was hurting you, it stopped being enjoyable for her. She couldn't bring herself to keep going when she learned you were not enjoying it. She thought that because you had had sex like that with each other in the past that it was still a green zone," Vanessa said in a way which made Loren wonder if it was her or Nancy talking. Vanessa opened her eyes to see Loren running from the lunch room.

Chapter 11

Am I stupid, believing in what some stranger has said, Loren thought as she packed her belongings in the Hotel room. She reached into her pocket and pulled out her phone. Nancy had messaged her every day, only to be left on read. Dialing her number, Loren waited impatiently for her to pick up.

"Hello Nancy's phone," Steff said, answering. Loren knew Steff would have seen her photo come up and knew very well who was ringing Nancy.

"Hi Steff, it's Loren, is...Mommy there?" Loren said, feeling her heart pound in her chest.

"No, she's not Loren. She's gone out with some friends and left her phone here. She's been staying with me since you left," Steff replied, clearly mad a Loren. Loren felt her stomach lurch. *Steff is such a cunt*; she thought to herself. As Loren was about to speak, she heard Nancy's voice asking who it was on the phone.

"Oh wrong number Nance," Steff said down the phone. Before Loren realized what she was saying she was yelling Mommy down the phone as loudly as she could, hoping Nancy would hear and hoping Steff's eardrum would be hurt.

"Baby?" Nancy said, taking the phone away from Steff.

"Mommy, I'm so sorry I ran away," Loren replied quickly, wanting Nancy to know it was her.

"Sweetheart, I've been so worried, you didn't even tell me where you were going," Nancy stated. Hearing the concern in her voice, Loren dropped to the floor and began to cry.

"I'm so sorry, I'm just so sorry," Loren said as she wept.

"No darling, I'm sorry. I made a huge mistake just assuming you would be OK with what I wanted to do to you just because we have done it before. I shouldn't have exhibited you like that. I didn't realize you wouldn't like it. Are you coming home to me baby girl?" Nancy said making Loren cry even more.

"You should be able to do whatever you want with me; I'm yours. I'm sorry I didn't let you do whatever," Loren said between sobs.

"That's not how I want our relationship to be baby. You're mine, but I don't want to hurt you, and I'm so sorry I did," Nancy said lovingly.

"My flight home is tomorrow, but I want to go to the airport and catch the first flight back. Will you pick me up, Mommy?" Loren asked, hoping Nancy would let her back into the house.

"Of course, tell me when your flight lands and I'll be there baby girl. Loren?" Nancy said seriously making Loren's eyes go wide.

"Yes, Mommy?" She replied curiously.

"Mommy will always be here for you baby girl. Mommy might make you mad, but you never need to run away from me, you can always come to me and say I've done something to upset you and we will talk about it until it's better," Nancy said making Loren's heart glow.

Nancy picked Loren up from the airport, and they held hands the whole car ride home. When Loren walked into the living room and put her bags down next to Nancy's couch, she smiled as she saw her bunny and blankie waiting for her. Loren turned around on the spot and Nancy pushed a pacifier into her mouth before she could say a word making her giggle.

"Has Mommy's baby girl missed this?" Nancy said, picking Loren up and carrying her into the nursery. Nancy took Loren's clothes off, grabbed a vibrator, butt plug and diaper, and walked into the bathroom and ran a bath for Loren who stayed in the nursery.

"Baby?" Nancy asked from the bathroom. When Loren entered, she was holding the paddle in one hand and her bunny by the ear in the other. Nancy raised an eyebrow and smirked.

"I guess you'll need this to Mommy," Loren said, handing the paddle to Nancy who took it and ran her fingers over it.

"You are very right baby, but Mommy is going to wait until tomorrow to punish you. Let's get you settled back in before I remind you who is boss. You aren't going to be doing another disappearing act on me, young lady," Nancy said playfully patting Loren's bottom and helping her into the bath. After Loren's bath Nancy lubed the toys and filled Loren's holes. Watching as she squirmed uncomfortably, Nancy laughed and picked Loren up for a hug.

"Mommy filled you up with the big toys today baby," Nancy said, pushing the butt plug in further making Loren limb with submission. Nancy fitted Loren into her diaper and turned the vibrator up, causing Loren to gasp and rub herself.

"No little one. You aren't allowed to touch," Nancy explained putting the remote into her back pocket and taking Loren's hands away. She took Loren's hand and led her back into the nursery and chose a white onesie, and pink socks, dressing Loren quickly while Loren squirmed and moaned as the vibrator kept her on the edge of orgasm. Nancy picked Loren up and cuffed her wrists and ankles to the cot. She took a pacifier gag from the draw and secured it around Loren's head and stroked Loren's forehead. Nancy then took a pink leather chastity belt from the cupboard fitted it tight over her onesie, making her diaper push firmly into her pussy.

"You better get used to that sweetheart. Mommy is going to keep you like that all night. I want you to fill that diaper with your sweet cum by morning. Welcome home little one," Nancy said as she turned off the light and closed the door behind her.

Who is Tina Moore?

Tina Moore has enjoyed the lifestyle of a Mommy Domme for several years. She began exploring kink and BDSM in her youth and found her love of being a strict Mommy Domme in early 2000. Tina Moore is now an author of many MDLG and ABDL themed novels.

Having enjoyed many years in the kink community, Tina Moore combines these experiences with the sweet and naughty things her baby girl does to bring you tantalizing and salacious stories.

Follow her on:

Author Page on Amazon

Instagram @tinamoore.kdp